The Goose Girl and the Artificial

A Goose Girl Retelling Novella

by

K M Robinson

THE GOOSE GIRL AND THE ARTIFICIAL
Copyright © 2018 by K.M. Robinson.

Published by Crescent Sea Publishing.
www.crescentseapublishing.com

Cover designed by Reading Transforms.
Image copyright © K.M. Robinson Photography.

This is a work of fiction. Names, characters, brands, trademarks, places, and incidents either are the product of the author's imagination or are used fictitiously. Any resemblance to actual events, locales, organizations, or persons, living or dead, is entirely coincidental and beyond the intent of either the author or the publisher.

All rights reserved, which includes the right to reproduce this book or portions thereof in any form whatsoever except as provided by the U.S. Copyright Law.

To Elle, without whom I never would have known the story of Goose Girl

"YOU DON'T HAVE A CHOICE," ARTA SNEERS. "YOU LOST your key—you have no control over me, and in case you've forgotten, I'm designed to be smarter than you."

My father always used to tell me that if I had to lose to someone, I should lose to someone that wasn't as smart as I was. That's hard advice to follow when the person you're losing to artificially *created* to be smarter than me.

I trail behind Arta as she walks away from Fal. My dress swishes behind her as she moves.

If they're smarter than you, they will know how to stay on top. If they aren't, you can beat them at their own game.

Arta is definitely smarter.

"Behave," I tap Fal on the head. He beeps quietly, slipping into sleep mode.

"Greetings," a man sings, walking swiftly toward us. "Thank you for making the journey. My son has been waiting for you."

"Thank you, your highness." Arta dips gracefully into a curtsy. "This is my Artificial."

She waves her hand at me.

"What might your name be?" the king asks.

"Goselyn, sir," I say softly. Arta waves a finger behind her back, reminding me to follow orders.

Artificials aren't required to bow to humans, so I hold my pose. There are a lot of things I'm going to have to remember to do now.

"Come along, ladies," the king turns, guiding us toward the massive palace.

Panels along the hallway walls mimic exterior windows, morphing into different scenes based on the king's biometric readings. The device around his neck reads his movements and controls the devices around him, including the settings on the fake windows.

A door slides back in front of us courtesy of the device, opening up into a stunning parlor. The walls are covered in red and gold tapestries—a stark contrast to the purple and silver in my own palace.

"Princess," a young man says, jumping to his feet as he

sets the book down he had been reading. "Thank you for coming all this way to handle the proposal."

Arta nods graciously to him.

"I think this will be a productive visit for us," she remarks, gathering her long skirt—*my* skirt—in her hand. "I'd like to freshen up after our journey if you don't mind. Perhaps we could begin our negotiations this evening?"

"Certainly, Princess Sylvane," he nods to her, referring to her by my official title. In Untae, the royals are referred to by their station and country as a way of identification. Outside of our own countries, people rarely know first names.

"You may call me Arta," my Artificial informs him as she swings around more gracefully than I ever could, and waltzes away. When I don't follow, she snaps my name.

We follow a short robot down several halls and up two flights of stairs before we step into Arta's room. Red floral curtains are drawn back to reveal the gardens in back of the palace.

"You may go," she dismisses the robot. It scurries back to its home base until it is needed again. "This is lovely…I can't wait to see it burn."

"They're going to figure this out, Arta," I protest. Her short dress around my calves frustrates me. In Sylvane, we distinguish humans from our recreations enhanced with artificial intelligence by wardrobe—though I'm considering changing that rule once I take over if this is what they have to suffer with every day. Then again, they can't feel the sensation of uncomfortable clothing, so perhaps that shouldn't be my first decision.

"They won't have time to figure it out, Goselyn. You yourself didn't realize what I was doing until after I had taken your key away. Do you really think a boy like that will figure out our plan? They're as easily replaced as you are—and just as unfit to preside over the countries of Untae.

"Your cousin has a plan, Goselyn," she addresses me as she sits on the bed. "Your kind cannot withstand it. The Artificals will keep this country functioning."

My cousin programs many of the palace Artificials. His work offers him access and power, but it's never been enough for him.

"By destroying this proposal?"

"We don't need Sylvane and Delare working together on this. Let's face it—neither country makes the best decisions," she reminds me. "Now go sit."

I make my way to the corner, settling on the small sofa where I will be sleeping for the length of our stay.

"Don't get any ideas about warning them either," Arta snaps. "You know I have your key—I can control anything I want back in Sylvane. Your mother is only safe as long as you cooperate."

"I understand the terms," I growl at my Artifical. "I'll

pretend to be you and let you destroy my reign in order to save my mother."

I glance down at the marble floor with its intricate pattern swirling into twists and turns. If only I could return home.

"Ridiculous diplomatic mission," I mumble under my breath. "I couldn't have just stayed home. *No, I* had to go and be the problem-solver and do my duty and traipse off to a far-off country to fulfill a silly little requirement before I can *eventually* take over the throne.

A knock sounds at the door. We both turn. Arta slices her hand in the air, motioning from me to the door—I'm the servant now.

I step back as I open the door. An Artificial stands outside holding a tray with a pitcher of water and two glasses. He steps inside and places it on the table.

"Prince Corinth will meet with you in half an hour downstairs in his office, Princess Sylvane." He nods to Arta. He turns to me. "You may come with me if the princess is no longer in need of your services."

"You may go, Goselyn. Do whatever they ask you to do and don't get in the way."

The Artifical leads me downstairs, past the parlor where we met Prince Corinth earlier. He wasn't bad looking—his height had surprised me a little since I had heard all of Delare was on the short side. I had heard he was rather brilliant, but I suppose I'll never find out.

The palace grounds are covered in flowers and stonework. Paths swirl as far as the eye can see. The Artifical leads me beyond the stables, toward the fountain.

"We don't have any real need for you, but you can assist here," he says, gesturing toward the lake. "The lake grounds are meant for enjoyment. The swans and geese are only permitted to get so close to the waterfront. You need to monitor the birds and keep them in their respective areas."

I nod, completely terrified. I have no idea how to keep large birds at bay.

"Gand is in charge here. Speak to him if you need anything."

A tall Artifical walks up to me imposingly. An Artifical would not flinch so I command my body to be still.

"You will monitor this area," he motions to his right. "This is how we handle the birds here."

He demonstrates the proper techniques for keeping the birds where they belong. One pecks him in anger, but he doesn't acknowledge it. This could create a problem for me as someone who *actually* feels pain.

I spend the rest of the day on a log, holding a Sheppard's hook to corral the geese with. As late afternoon arrives, Gand chases the birds back inside a building where they are fed and sheltered at night.

I don't understand the purpose of having the creatures if they're going to shut them up every night. Why not spare the entire area and set them free off of the palace grounds?

I settle back into a standing position near a log, waiting for the birds to attack.

We take our meals inside Arta's room—*my* room—to avoid prying eyes. Artificals do not need to eat and Arta skipping meals while I indulged would raise flags.

A week goes by as I sit with the geese and swans, prodding them away when they get too close.

"May I ask you a question?" a voice asks one afternoon.

Prince Corinth takes a seat on the log next to me, fidgeting with his hands.

"Yes, Prince Delare, of course."

My hand migrates toward my hair, but I quickly force it back into my lap. I can't risk moving my locks and exposing my neck. If he notices I don't have a control panel with a chip, he will figure out what has happened.

I silently think of ten vicious names to call my cousin when I return home, though none of them are strong enough to convey how angry I am at him for trying to take my throne and putting my mother in danger.

"You may call me Corinth. I'm sorry, what was your

name again?"

"I'm Goselyn, sir." I keep my eyes transfixed on the ground, hoping he will go away.

"Goselyn. Right," he reminds himself. "Goselyn, I was wondering if you could give me any advice on working with Princess Arta. She and I seem to be having trouble connecting over this proposal."

"What do you mean?"

"Well, every time I think we have something worked out, she seems to hesitate. I keep thinking that I'm saying the right things, but then she seems to get frustrated with me.

"I know we both want this to work—it *has* to work for either of to complete our requirements for taking the next step toward the throne—but I'm worried we're never going to reach an agreement."

"I don't have any advice for you, I'm afraid," I reply sadly. "She has a specific plan in mind."

One designed by my cousin. I'm not sure how he overrode Arta's original programming, but he manipulated her into turning on me.

"I see." He frowns, rubbing his fingers over his temple. "Perhaps you could tell me about Sylvane? Maybe that would offer me some insight."

"Shouldn't you be negotiating with the princess?" I attempt to get him to go back to the palace.

"We're taking a break. We don't seem to be getting

anywhere today."

"Surely your father could help you," I comment, silently pleading for them to figure it out and help disable my Artificial.

"He's not allowed to take part in the negotiations. The princess and I are the only two allowed to work on it and whatever we come up with is final…she can't even leave until it's done," he mutters, frustrated with Arta's hesitance. "I'm sure you're ready to go home, Goselyn—it's been an entire week. Can you just try to think of something that will help me?"

"Sir, they're looking for you," an Artificial approaches us, waving toward the palace.

"Perhaps we could speak tomorrow," the prince says as he stands. He strides toward the palace, sending a group of geese scattering toward me.

"What did he want?" Gand asks, wandering over to help push the geese back.

"Advice for working with the princess."

"Did you give it to him?" He pushes at a swan. It flaps its wings dangerously.

"I have nothing to give—the princess makes up her own mind over things."

"How many years have you worked with her?"

I gently bump the chest of a white goose with the end of my hook, trying to coax it back before Gand can reach it.

"Many," I reply. He pauses to evaluate what I said.

"You've been studying her this long and you don't have any insight on how to handle her?" he inquires. "Perhaps in Sylvane, the technological advances are not as great. Here in Delare, we know everything there is to know about the humans, down to how their facial expressions will change based on the food that they eat. I do not believe you have no information about your princess."

"I know many things about her," I fire back. "I simply have nothing that will help the prince convince her of things she does not wish to do."

"You've been here a week," Gand replies, taking a step closer. "In that time, you have worked alongside of me here with the birds. You don't act like a normal Artificial, but I cannot decide if it is because Artificials are different where you are from or if you are here for another reason."

"I do not know if we are different. I only know this is how I am," I inform him, trying not to get caught in a conversation.

"I'm watching you," he says, turning his back to walk back to his own area.

Arta is going to be thrilled—the local Artificials could bring her plan down before I do.

Gand studies me from afar as I pretend not to notice.

The moment we are released from our duties, I walk back to the palace and head straight for my room.

"About time," Arta says.

"The prince says you're being difficult," I confront her.

"Well of course I am—this isn't supposed to be easy. He has to be willing to give in just to get this thing finished."

"Oh, so *that's* your plan? Wear him down until he agrees to anything?" I kick my shoes off as I walk to my sofa in the corner. Draping a blanket over my feet, I compensate for the short dress I'm wearing.

"Yes, it is," she glares as she walks across the room. "Now eat, that. I was supposed to have the tray set out twenty minutes ago."

She motions to the food on the small table. I race to it quickly, piling as much food as I could onto a napkin. I take several bites out of the apple before setting it back on the tray and leave bits of the pastry crumbled on the plate before setting it outside the door to be picked up.

At least Arta wasn't depriving me of food.

"Now stay here. I have to attend a ceremony in the rose garden and I don't need you getting in the way."

She glides across the room toward the door.

"I don't know why these silly ceremonies are so

important to you humans. Traditions are ridiculous, especially when they have to do with flowers."

She marches out of the room as the door swings shut.

I grab the sheets I smuggled into the room yesterday from under the sofa cushions. Tying them to the handle on the window probably isn't my best move, but I have to get out of the palace without her knowing and the other Artificials can easily see me from the hallway.

I'm only a floor off of the ground, but it's still enough to make my stomach drop when I look over the ledge. I slip my shoes into my dress pockets before carefully swinging myself out the window.

After an eternity, I reach the ground. I didn't inherit many things from my father, but my hand-eye coordination is the thing I appreciate the most. Aiming, I throw my smuggled knife high into the air, praying it's enough to slice through the sheet I braided into a rope. Part of it rips before the knife falls back to the earth.

I jump back to avoid the falling blade. Once it settles and no longer bounces against the ground, I rush to the sheet-rope. I pull on it, trying to break it free. The material rips, but not enough. Using my full weigh, I jump up to grab it, using gravity to my advantage.

It breaks.

My feet don't cooperate as I fall, leaving me in a pile on the ground. The braided sheet hits me in the head and I bit my tongue to keep from snarling at it.

The bush acts as a hiding place for the evidence of my escape—I'll need to find a new way back inside, but at least they didn't see my leave from the hallways.

If I can find Fal, I can send him to my mother with a message. Arta has been keeping me from my loyal butler, refusing to let me see him.

I creep around the side of the castle, making sure no one is there. When I'm sure it's clear, I run toward the stables where everything that didn't come with us to the room is being stored.

Our vehicle sits at the far end of the stable, away from the animals. I tiptoe as quietly as I can through the array of animals, grateful I haven't put my shoes back on yet. Any noise might spook the creatures.

I quietly open the door, looking to see where Fal might be. I had put him into sleep mode so he shouldn't have gone far.

I tear the vehicle apart, having no luck finding him. I final extricate myself from the vehicle, stepping out backward onto the dirt.

A distant beep pierces the air so softly that I'm not sure I heard it at all. I turn slowly, trying to locate the source. When I can't find it, I close the door and begin to move around the stable, looking for where Fal might be hidden—I won't let Delare steal my butler.

I jump out of my skin when I hear the beep again, this

time overhead. My eyes sweep over the walls until I finally spot him.

Mounted on the wall high above me is Fal's head. I shriek, clamping my hand over my mouth to try to stifle the noise.

Fal's body is nowhere to be found. A string of lights blink across his eyes, adding the only color to Fal's silver shape. Without the rest of him, he looks like an upside-down metal bowl that blinks.

"Fal," I whisper.

He hovers somewhere between sleep mode and functioning mode, just enough to make small noises and move the tiny lights across his face. I reach up, tapping his head. I struggle on my toes to stretch high enough.

When I tap him, his eye light up, white with blue electronic pupils, as he connects with my biometric signature.

"Goselyn," he says quietly. "They took me apart."

"What happened to you?" I can feel myself on the verge of tears as I lower my heels down to the ground.

"Arta didn't want me to tell the Delare royalty what had happened. She had them dismantle me—she told them I wasn't functioning properly. They took my body and gave it to another robot and put my central system up here until they can reprogram me."

"We can't let them reprogram you!" I shout.

As a robot, Fal's programming does not allow the

Artificials to have access to him, but it also means that if someone reprograms him, he will be gone for good—robots' systems are far less complex and advanced than Artificials' systems.

"What is she trying to do?" His eyes light up, changing color.

A noise on the other side of the stable stops us. Fal dims his lights, going into his night state. I press against the wall, hiding behind a barrel. After a few moments, the person leaves.

"What does she want, Goselyn?" Fal repeats from his place on the wall.

"She's trying to ruin the negotiations and change the proposal. My cousin reprogrammed her because he wants me out of the picture. He thinks by destroying this proposal, I won't be allowed to succeed my mother and it will fall to his family."

"You need to tell your mother," Fal informs me as if I didn't know.

"That's why I was trying to find you. You're the only one that can get back to Sylvane without Arta finding out."

"I can't move without my body." Fal's face lights up with green, red, and yellow dots racing across his inter-face. He beeps unintentionally as his system flails from being mounted on the wall.

"I couldn't even get you down if I tried." I look around

for something to climb on to reach him.

"I'm stuck up here. Even if you could reach me, it would take an hour to get me unhooked. There's something weird back here." His lights slow to a crawl. "You need to go back and find a way to warn the king. You know if your cousin is coming after you, he will also go after Delare—he's always said he should take command here if you were to inherit Sylvane."

Another noise frightens us across the stable.

"Just go, Goselyn. Put me in sleep mode and come back after you've ended this. I'll be fine."

"But—" I protest.

"No. You need to go. I can't help you. You need to put Sylvane first."

Fal has always been wise beyond his programming.

"I'll be back for you," I promise as I reach up to turn on his sleep mode setting.

"I'm sure you will. Good luck, Goselyn." He beeps when I tap him, settling into sleep mode.

Stopping Arta before Fal is reprogrammed becomes my second motivation for beating my Artificial, urging me to quickly sneak out of the stables. I slip my shoes on once I reach the grass and hurry toward the palace.

The most dangerous part of my return journey into the palace is slipping by the kitchen without being noticed. People bustle about, preparing the evening meal. I can smell the roast chicken from down the hall.

"What are you doing?"

I jump at the question. Spinning, I clutch my chest. Artificials shouldn't be scared, but I can't help my reaction.

"Goselyn, what are you doing?" Grad demands. His jaw clenches like a real human's would. "I knew it—you're not an Artificial."

"No, I am," my words come out panicked and high-pitched.

"You're not," he says, reaching for my neck. He struggles to move my hair as I fight back.

As we grapple, I do my best to eject the chip from the back of his neck. The Artificial throws me against the wall, slamming me between it and the back of his shoulder. I yelp in pain.

I stomp on his foot, causing him to look down long enough to punch the button on the back of his neck. It pops out just enough for his face to go slack.

Opening the small control panel, I pull up his programming. While I only learned a few things from my father, I gained many skills from my mother, including the ability to alter the programming of the Artificials and robots we work with.

Before securing the chip back in place, I program Gand to not be able to come within ten feet of me. I also erase the last ten minutes of his memory. He will know I removed the time from his programming, but it will take him a few days to recover it, giving me enough time to fix the problem with Arta—*I hope*.

While Gand blinks back to life, I slip down the hall and dart around the corner. I make it back to my room with just enough time to pull the remnant of the sheet off the window and close it before Arta opens the door. She eyes me but says nothing.

The next day, I make my way down to the lake, the geese following in my wake. Gand watches me from his place on the other side of the lawn, trying to figure out what happened.

I turn my shoulder away, keeping my back to him as I corral the birds on the lawn.

"Gand," the prince's voice bounces off a nearby tree. I look up in time to see Gand retreating, having been dangerously close to me.

"Should I ask what that was about?" Corinth asks as he sits next to me on the log. His blond hair tips down gently over one eye as he turns to face me.

I pull my dark hair over my neck, ensuring he can't see my skin.

"I don't know," I try to keep my response simple.

"Have you thought of anything that might help me?" he asks. I sigh.

"Perhaps…" I pause, trying to think of *anything* I can give him. "Let her think she has won. Give in to as much as you can, but hold true to the most important things and make them seem unimportant. If she thinks she has won, perhaps you can make this work."

"That's an interesting thought," Corinth replies. "I'll try that. You're very wise, Goselyn. I knew I liked you."

He stands, preparing to leave.

"How do you like it here, Goselyn? Are you finding everything to your liking?" he asks, turning back to me.

"Delare is a very nice country, sir."

"Thank you," he smiles. "That's not what I meant."

"I'm doing fine, thank you."

I'm only being held captive by an artificial who is threatening the lives of everyone around me at the whims of my narcissistic cousin, but sure, I'm great.

"Is Gand treating you well?" he inquires, putting his hand behind his back as he was trained to do.

I smile, not wanting to answer.

"Gand?" Corinth calls, motioning my keeper over. "How has everything been? Are you two working together well?"

"Goselyn has been managing just fine, Prince Corinth."

"Very good," he replies, giving Gand a curious look. "You're taking care of her, right? Treating her as one of our own?"

"Yes, sir," Gand assures him, placing his free hand on his Sheppard's hook in an attempt to make the prince feel more at ease. Artificials are trained to make human-like movements specifically to make humans feel more comfortable around them, even to the point of regularly blinking.

"Good, we want everyone to feel welcome here," Corinth smiles, nodding to me. It's amazing how he takes so much time to talk to his Artificials publicly. I've had many long talks with mine, but only in private.

Gand takes a step toward us. He suddenly leaps back as if a bee stung him. Corinth looks as shocked as Gand does.

"Are you all right?" Corinth moves toward him.

Gand's eyes shift toward the clouds as he processes what just happened.

"I…I'm not sure what that was." He takes another step forward, bouncing back as if he's hit a wall. Gand won't know it until he recovers the data I deleted, but I programmed him to do that.

"Perhaps you should come inside and have one of the programmers take a look," Corinth reaches a hand toward the Artificial. "Maybe there's a glitch in your data."

Unable to resist, Gand follows him toward the palace.

"Will you be okay on your own, Goselyn?" The prince

turns back to me with a concerned look on his face, brow furrowed kindly.

"Yes." What other choice do I have? At least Gand won't be in my hair today.

I take a seat as the prince and the Artificial walk away. For a moment, I consider letting the geese roam free for a while, but I don't need any extra questions. I go back to tending them properly.

It isn't long before Arta joins me.

"What happened?" she demands.

"The Artificial was asking too many questions. He got close to me and I managed to pop his chip out and program him to stay away from me so that he didn't expose your little plan."

She grimaces, wrinkling her nose.

"Fine. Keep it that way. I'm nearly done anyway."

"You mean we'll get to go home?" I ask, standing.

"Yes. I just have to get the prince to sign the proposal and then I can remove him."

My blood runs cold.

"What do you mean?"

"Oh stop being so sentimental, Goselyn. I won't do it while we're here. We still have to go home, present the proposal, enact the plan, and *then* we'll kill him—you don't have to watch any of it. All you have to do is keep your mouth shut."

Before my cousin got his hands on her, Arta never

would have spoken to me like that.

My knee pops out of place, nearly forcing me to pitch forward. Arta's eyes grow wide for a moment before narrowing.

"Pull it together," she hisses. Any human-like movements could give us away—Artificials don't let their knees pop. She blinks intentionally, compensating for her lack of human motions.

"Princess," the king calls from the hill. "My son is waiting for you inside. He'd like you to join him in his study if you don't mind."

My first reaction is to curtsy, but I remember just in time and manage to hold still. I wait as Arta accepts his initiation to return to the palace.

Part way up the hill, the king slows. Once Arta is safely inside, he returns to me.

"Hello," he greets me. He's friendlier than his son, though, I imagine, just as strategic.

"Hello, King Delare."

"All by yourself today?" He stands with his hands behind his back, posture straight as my Sheppard's hook.

"Your son sent Gand in to be looked at my a programmer. He seemed to be experiencing a glitch," I report.

"Yes, I caught him on the way out actually. Had quite the story to tell," he pauses, removing a hand from behind his back to stroke his chin. "It seems he thinks you are not an Artificial. I wonder why he would think that..."

"I don't know, sir." I look down, trying to avoid him as I scoot a goose back.

"I see," the king muses. "And there's nothing you would like to tell me?"

"No, sir."

He pauses, trying to decide what to say next. A swan wanders by us but he waves for me to leave it alone.

A few dozen yards away, the fountain cascades into itself, creating a never-ending cycle of soothing sound. I wonder if I could hide behind it.

"Perhaps it's that you *can't* tell me." The king tips his head, examining me.

"I couldn't say, sir," I reply.

"I see," the king says solemnly. "Maybe you'd like to sit with me."

He motions me over to the log. He's larger than his son and takes up more space on the turned tree stump.

"I would very much like to help you, Goselyn, but I can't do that unless I know what is going on. No one is watching us and your princess is behind closed doors. All of my Artificials, robots, and workers have been removed from the area. If something is going on, now is the time to tell me," he insists. He's clearly trying to be gentle with me, but the wrinkles on his forehead suggest that he's worried something is going on.

I don't trust Arta. She decapitated Fal—or order him to be. She's threatening my mother. Even just now, she told me she's planning the assassination of a ruling monarch of another country. The king may feel it is safe, but I know it is not.

"I truly do not know what you mean, sir." I reach up, brushing back my hair. Pulling it to one side, I expose the skin on my neck.

"I see," the king says slowly, eyes widening. "And you're sure there is nothing I can help you with?"

"I think the only thing you can do, sir, is help your son. He's in greater need of it than I am," I say, praying he understands my meaning. I tip my head to emphasize my point. "Children need their parents to look after them just as much as parents need their children protecting them."

"You make a good point," he agrees, standing. "I'll see to my son. He's always been good about keeping secrets, as I'm sure your Princess Arta is.

"I hear you've been advising my son. Thank you for your help. I'm sure he would like to thank you personally later." He makes it ten feet before he turns back to me. "I think I shall send a letter to your queen, thanking her for the magnificent representatives she has sent for this diplomatic mission. I'm sure she'll be quite pleased to hear of it."

"I'm sure it would mean everything to her, thank you. You'll want to send that via Channel One so no one accidentally intercepts it."

"Indeed," he nods, acknowledging that he understands someone else is controlling this scenario—no Artificial would have knowledge of the private communication channels of the reigning monarchs. Not even my cousin knows about it—only the kings, queens, and crowned princes and princesses know of its existence.

The king of Delare is willing to warn my mother of my cousin's plans. I want to throw my arms around him to thank him, but I hold still. My mother will know what to do to disable Arta's ability to control the Artificial in Sylvane the moment she reads his communication—now I just have to figure out how to survive Delare and return to take down my cousin.

"Princess," Corinth greets me by my title, corning me outside the stable. I eye him warily until he holds up a necklace—a device that prohibits intelligence gathering within a certain radius. It knocks out all cameras and recording devices while looping in old footage. "We're alone."

"Has your father contacted my mother?" I ask.

"He has. I'm so sorry you had to go through all of this. Your mother is working to shut down Arta's ability to control the Artificials as we speak. She'll be safe soon."

I hope she figured out that my cousin is behind this

and didn't enlist his help. We've always been wary of his demands and outbursts, so I'm sure she's being cautious.

"You're in danger," I quickly tell the prince. "Arta is planning to destroy the proposal, and then once it's public, she's going to remove you."

"Remove me?" His eyes widen as he takes a step back. "What does that mean?"

"I assume it means you're going to die," I try to say gently. "My cousin wants my throne *and* yours, so he's trying to take us both out at once after we've returned with the proposal."

"But if she's not here, how will she manage that?"

"I would imagine that she's not the only Artificial in on this plan." I glance around, waving him into the shadows of the building. "It's entirely possible he has control of some of *your* Artificials too.

"Gand must not know, or he wouldn't have pushed things with me, but who knows which of them are working together on this."

"Why is he doing this—other than simply wanting the thrones?"

"My cousin believes his leadership would be superior, Corinth—he doesn't think we can handle ruling. He doesn't want our countries working together."

"We've done just fine until now," he says bitterly.

"Now we just have to prove it."

Corinth nods to me as I trail behind Arta into the parlor —my mother has sent word back that she is safe.

Let the games begin.

"Princess, have a seat," Corinth motions toward a fainting couch with a large, ornate gold rim along the tiny fragment of a back.

Arta arranges her skirt carefully as she sits. I quietly follow behind her, taking a seat on the edge of the couch, prepared to go after her control panel if needed.

"I've been thinking about a few addendums to the proposal," Corinth starts. He lays out a few papers on their laps as he sits next to her. "I think it would be beneficial if we could—"

"What is this?" Arta shrieks. She gathers the papers up and shoves them at the prince. "No, we agreed to the original proposal and we're sticking to that."

"No, actually we didn't, princess. You tried to *force* me into it, but you never once listened to me. This is what I feel we need to add to make this beneficial to Delare and not just Sylvane," he protests, trying to hand her the paperwork again.

"You are a fool," Arta shakes her head in disgust. "I will leave right now and neither of us will have completed our part of the proposal."

"You can't be queen without it," he reminds Arta,

jumping to his feet to follow behind her as she sprints toward the door. "But honestly, *I* don't mind. I've never really had a taste for ruling. You'd be doing me a favor."

Arta looks at him in shock.

"This hurts *you* more than it hurts me, Arta," he says in a darker voice. "If you want me to play along, you have to make this worth my time. You've offered me nothing."

Arta pauses, her face going slack, as she processes the information, a telltale sign that she's an Artificial. When she comes out of it, she blinks.

"I can offer you my hand in marriage. We can rule our countries together."

"No, thank you, you're not my type," Corinth quickly replies, infuriating her.

"Well, what do you want?" she demands.

"A robot, for starters." He grins. "I hear you had one brought here. I'd like to see it. Your robots are quite a bit different than ours here in Delare, so it would be a bit of a novelty."

"It's broken." Her words are biting.

"It's not," he challenges her. "I saw you bring it in. Go fetch it."

He waves his hand at her, shooing her toward the tall, oak door. Arta looks like a petulant child about to stamp their foot.

"Goselyn," she shrieks my name, never taking her eyes off of the prince.

"Let's all go," Corinth encourages, motioning for me to quickly follow.

Atra argues the entire way down the hall that she doesn't know where Fal is, but Corinth expertly guides her toward the stables where he knows our things are being stored.

"There he is," I add when we can finally see my butler strung up on the wall.

"What happened to him?" Corinth yells, acting surprised.

"I told you, he was broken. Your programmers took him apart for scraps."

"You're not handing me a robot head," Corinth snarls. "Go find it a body."

He swings back to face me, away from Arta.

"This is ridiculous," he growls at me with a playful wink. He turns back around to face her. "Well?"

Arta huffs and scurries off to find Fal's missing pieces.

"That will keep her busy for a while," Corinth grins as he steps toward me.

"Oh?" I try not to blush as he smirks at me.

"I hid the pieces," he shrugs. His eyes sparkle when he notices my cheeks and he quirks an eyebrow at me. "She's going to have to make him a body from scratch. I think we should follow her and see what she does."

He tugs at my hand, keeping a safe distance behind Arta as she scours the stables for anything she can use to recreate Fal. She throws things behind her, disrupting the animals, but she doesn't flinch even once as they panic.

We follow her through the stables, out into the yard as she stomps around, looking for anything she can use to cobble together a robot body. She never once considered asking me to do the work for her, though she's also aware that I don't have the technical skills to build a robot body.

A vicious tug pulls me back as we stride toward the palace. I shriek against my captor, fighting to break free. Corinth wheels around, ready to defend me.

"She is not an Artificial," Gand rages, pulling me away from Corinth.

"I know, let her go, Gand," the prince commands. "Now!"

Gand freezes, still holding me against his silicone body covered in lab-created skin. The only thing that gives him away is his lack of pulse.

"Sir, she does not belong here. She is lying to us. She needs to be taken for questioning." His grip tightens around me.

If I had seen him coming, I could have defended myself, but Artificials can be as much as three times stronger than a human. I wriggle under his grasp. Even Corinth looks slightly worried.

"Put her down, Gand. I'm aware of what is going on." Corinth lowers his hand, indicating that I should be set down.

The moment my feet touch the ground, I sprint toward the prince, pushing away from Gand.

"She erased my memory, Prince Corinth," Gand addresses him. "She attacked me in the hallway and tried to undo my programming."

"No, Gand. You attacked her and she was trying to protect herself *and* me. I can't explain it now, but you'll understand soon."

"I will take this to your father," Gand threatens.

"He already knows, Gand."

The Artificial takes a dangerous step toward the crowned prince of Delare. Corinth doesn't back down.

"Go back to the geese, Gand." Corinth reaches for the key around his neck, prepared to force Gand back.

The Artifical turns around slowly, slinking back toward the lake. We watch as he kicks at several of the geese.

"You need to find him a new job," I comment, pursing my lips.

"Or to turn down his anger levels," Corthin murmurs back.

"Maybe take out his personality all together?" I suggest earning a smug, close-lipped grin as Corinth fights not to laugh.

"But he has such a charming personality," he remarks.

"True. The Artificials of Delare are so welcoming." I toss my hair as I speak, rolling my eyes dramatically.

"Hey, we're not all bad," Corthin corrects me.

"I didn't realize you were an Artificial. I supposed that would explain why you weren't friendlier to me," I tease.

"I wasn't the one concealing my identity, princess," he reminds me casually. "We should catch up to Arta."

With the sudden change in conversation, we spin around and hurry back toward the palace, assuming Arta went inside to look for supplies.

It's quiet inside as we search for Arta, methodically sweeping the rooms until we locate her. The loud crash in the dining hall suggests we've found her.

When we enter, it's not Arta, but rather the king that we see first.

"Son," he warns in a harsh tone. "Get back."

Arta's arm is wrapped around his neck. She grabs her wrist, using her forearm to apply pressure to the king's throat. He struggles uncomfortably beneath her grasp. Corinth gasps beside me.

"Arta," I try to reason with her, though I'm not sure why since she's under my cousin's control. "Let him go. There's still a way to make this work."

"How is that?" she asks, her programming urging her to listen.

"We can still get both parties to sign the proposal. You and I can still take it back to Sylvane," I reply, taking a small step toward her.

"It's too late for that—they already know about the plan," Arta contradicts me.

"They only know what you've told them," I assure her.

"Don't lie, Goselyn," she gives me a withering look. "You've never been good at it."

"Can he hear us?" I ask, referring to my cousin in Sylvane.

She pauses, waiting for confirmation. Finally, she nods.

"Kenneth," I call. "You need to end this. We won't hold it against you if you stop now."

Arta drops her arm from around the king's neck. His hands fly to his throat as he attempts to step away from the Artificial.

The moment of hope passes as Arta runs full speed at me. Corinth attempts to block her, only resulting in him being pushed to the ground.

My Artificial tackles me to the ground, our screams mixing together. Something twitches in her eyes as we wrestle-perhaps a bit of the old Arta before she was reprogrammed. She slams my head into the ground.

I kick her off of me, sitting up to a spinning world. Corinth throws himself on her, forcing her backward until she tosses him over her shoulder.

The king runs at Arta at full speed, slamming her into the wall with his shoulder. She grunts, struggling to get her footing while she claws at his face.

I hate the idea of hurting my Artificial, but she's no longer the Arta I know—she's something much more hideous now at the hands of my cousin.

Art breaks free of the king as Artificials pour into the room to see what is happening. They surround us for a moment, looking on.

I pause next to Corinth, breathing just as heavily as he is. We watch the group of human-like creations as they watch us, unsure of who has control.

The king hits his button to protect himself from the Artificials.

"Son," he warns, urging the prince to enable his key to protect himself.

"She doesn't have one," Corinth replies, refusing to enable his safety net if it will leave me vulnerable.

The king looks equally as shocked as he looks over-whelmed with respect for his son.

"I think you two are going to get along just fine after this," he murmurs. "But we really don't have time for this right now."

He rushes at Arta, slamming his elbow into her face. Her head snaps back at an angle so sharp that it would have done incredible damage had she not been a machine.

"Get the key," he demands as he pushes his hand against her face to hold Arta back.

We scramble forward, unsure if our movements will

cause the Artificials to attack. Corinth tears at Arta's neck, looking for the chain my key is on.

I could help Corinth and retrieve my key, but that will only protect us for so long. Instead, I thrust my hands toward the back of Arta's neck, fumbling for her control panel.

"That won't work," she warns me. "You can't eject my chip. Kenneth made sure."

I would eject her chip if I had to shatter her neck to do it.

"I'm smarter than my cousin," I counter.

"He's a programmer," she yelps, struggling to rip my hands away. "He's better than you."

"We both had the same teacher," I respond, fingers slipping off her fake skin. "I promise you my mother didn't teach him everything she taught me."

Arta uses her feet to push off the wall as the Artificials erupt around us, some breaking free of whatever control Kenneth had over them, while others are still clearly under his programming.

The king falls to the ground, nearly tripping Arta. She springs over him at the last second, leaving me only a step behind her. I tackle her, attempting to pin her arms.

"Use your key," I scream at Corinth.

"I didn't get yours yet," he yells back, rushing to my side.

"You need to stay protected," I shout back.

"So do you, *princess*," he says, for the first time, not using my title respectfully.

"One thing at a time, *prince*."

I lower myself, running at Arta. Grabbing her around the waist, we topple to the ground. I pull open the control panel on her neck, prepared to punch in the necessary information to fight back against my cousin.

Corinth throws himself on top of us, lending his weight to the struggle. He rips my key necklace from around her throat a he sits on the Artificial.

He gently leans toward me, brushing back my hair as he wraps the small digital key rectangle around my neck, latching it. He twists the clasp around to the back of my neck, tickling me in the process.

I reach up for a moment to enable the biometric key, knowing Corinth can't do it for me. As soon as it locks into place, putting a digital barrier between me and the rest of the fighting, I go back to my attempts to disable my Artificial.

"Anytime, Goselyn," Corinth says as he pitches forward. Arta bucks, trying to throw us off. He catches me, holding me steady as I work.

"Kenneth," I lecture my Artificial sharply, knowing my cousin is getting a full report. "You're going to pay for this."

"Goselyn," the king shouts, running to our sides. "A bot just arrived with a message. "Your mother has control of your cousin. All you have to do is reset your Artificial."

The news gives me renewed strength. I lunge at Arta again, working to key in the proper codes to disable the override. She struggles, but there isn't much she can do under the weight of two of us.

I key in the final commands and she goes slack. We sit in silence.

"Is it over?" Corinth finally asks, afraid to move.

"It's over," I breathe, shuffling off of the motionless Artificial. "You should also have control over your Artificials again."

I motion toward the human-like figures around us. They've already slowed, connecting to their former programming.

"Already taken care of, my dear," the king replies. "I think it's time you contacted your mother."

"And time to get the proposal negotiations back on track," Corinth adds. "I get the feeling that we really shouldn't wait on that."

"I agree," I let out a nervous laugh. "But first, can we go get Fal, please?"

"I'm sure you need something to feel a little more secure about your place here," the king responds. "Corinth, take the princess to rescue her robot, please."

Corinth offers me a hand. Together, we leave Arta's shell on the floor. The king's Artificials will take her to their programmer to get her back up and running in her former working condition before I leave, though, I imagine I'll have some trouble trusting her for a while.

"I'm sorry we made you work with the geese," Corinth drawls as we walk toward the stables. He places his hand behind his back properly.

"There were swans there too," I remind him. "Aren't we past all the formal stuff at this point?"

He smiles slightly, not missing a step.

"I suppose we are, Goselyn." He drops his arm, walking more casually. "I do apologize that you had to go through all this though. I'm sure it was very difficult."

"I'm sorry I brought it all to you. I didn't have any idea until right before we arrived," I sigh.

"It's not your fault," he says as we approach the tall doors to the barn. "I think I might have a few things to say to your cousin though."

He chuckles warmly.

"Well, perhaps you'll have to come give him a piece of your mind."

"I might have to." He walks a little faster, catching the door to hold it open for me. "After you."

Fal is sitting on the wall where I left him, still in sleep mode.

"Hold on," Corinth says as I reach for my robot.

He finds a step stool in the very back and drags it over. Climbing up, he wrestles Fal's central system off the wall. A programmer joins us, carrying Fal's body. He expertly puts him back together, though the wait is excruciating.

I tap Fal's head, bringing him back to life. The light blinks on, simulating eyes as colors dart across the interface.

"You did it?" Fal asks, beeping the way a cat might purr.

"We got word to mother and she helped us turn of Kenneth's programming. They're working on fixing Arta now."

Fal notices Corinth and beeps at him.

"He's fine, Fal," I smile. "Corinth, this is my robot, Fal. Fal, this is Prince Corinth of Delare."

"Nice to meet you, Fal." Corinth looks like he wants to get down on his knees and address the robot as a child. My robot beeps back at him.

"Your Highness," Fal addresses him.

"I'm sorry about the rude welcome. I hope you'll allow us to fix that," Corinth apologizes.

Fal looks up to me, gauging my reaction. I nod, encouraging him to relax.

"We have negotiations to work on," I redirect the conversation. "We should probably get back. I need to message my mother too."

"Of course, Princess."

"You're much easier to work with," Corinth informs me as a tray overflowing with fruits and cheeses is set on the table next to us. "Prettier too, if I might add."

My hand stops in mid-air as I blush profusely.

"You like doing that, don't you?" I ask, blinking back the uncertainty.

"Making you squirm? Yes," he answers bluntly.

"That nice guy act was just for show, huh?" I pick up a grape.

"Oh no, I'm always nice to the Artificials—they don't do so well with sarcasm and flirtation."

"I liked you better when I was an Artificial," I tease.

"Most people do," he nods innocently. "The good news is that we're almost done with these charges against your cousin, so you can go home soon and never see me again."

"You say that as if you weren't planning on coming along to harass Kenneth during his trial," I mumble, glancing up just in time to catch his grin. He quickly rearranges his face to hide it.

"Fine, you'll be rid of me after I see justice is done. You'll be sad to see me go though."

"Will I?"

"You will," Fal beeps next to me. I quickly tap him on

the head, putting him into sleep mode. Corinth smirks, scooting closer on the couch.

"I like the little guy," he shrugs casually. "I also like that I don't have to be so proper around you."

"Benefits of fighting an insane Artificial together, I suppose."

"What would you have done," he asks, putting his arm on the back of the couch, "if my father hadn't found out you weren't an Artificial."

"Climbed out the window again and escaped, I suppose."

He looks as though I've struck him.

"You climbed out the window?

"Did I not tell you about that part? Oops," I shrug, reaching for another grape.

He catches it out of my fingers, popping it into his mouth.

"That's what happens when you keep things from me," he informs me.

"It's been a week—we hardly know each other well enough to share all of our secrets," I retort.

"Two weeks, madam," he corrects, staring at my hand resting on my knee.

"Yes, but only one of being a human."

"Fine, I'll give you that, goose girl. Good thing we have the entire journey to Sylvane to talk."

"Oh, doesn't that sound lovely?"

"It does." He purses his lips, tipping his head as he looks at me.

"Goose girl?" I question.

"Yeah," he grins. "Since you like pecking at me so much—"

"Your Highnesses," a knock at the door sounds. "We've fixed her."

The programmer opens the door, stepping to the side. Arta stands beside him quietly.

"Your mother sent us the specifications," the programmer informs us. "She's been restored to her last backup."

"Hello, Goselyn."

I tap Fal on the head much harder than anticipated. He springs to life, wheeling himself over to inspect Arta.

I reach up, taping my key necklace to control my Artificial. After going through the motions of testing her, I finally release Arta.

"Welcome back, friend."

She smiles at me as I introduce her to Prince Corinth.

Corinth recoils as she turns an icy glare on him when I inform her that the prince will be traveling with us. I'm positive this will be a very enlightening trip home.

ACKNOWLEDGMENTS

Thank you, dear reader, for coming on this journey with me. The Goose Girl and the Artificial was originally written for an anthology (thus why it's so short) and I'm thrilled to release it as a standalone.

I hadn't actually heard of this story until Elle Beaumont mentioned it to me when I was looking for a topic for this retelling. I read the original story and was a little appalled by some of what I had read—beheading a horse and then having it talk while mounted to a wall was a bit shocking—but it gave me the incentive to figure out how to not be so horrifying when Fal was cut to pieces. I knew the only way I'd be okay decapitating Fan was if he weren't an actual animal, which resulted in him becoming a robot, which then inspired the artificial intelligence angle of the story.

Special thanks to Elle for sending the original Goose Girl story my way, and to J.M. for letting me talk through my thoughts until I figured out the robot and artificial intelligence angle.

Thanks to Jess and Elissa for their continued help getting my typos into shape.

I hope you all enjoyed this twisted take on the Goose Girl story. If you haven't read the original, I encourage you to check it out—it's a very interesting read and I think I did a pretty good job keeping true to the original and giving some pretty cool nods to it in this version of the story.

Stay inspired!

-K.M. Robinson

WORLD PORTALS

Ready to learn exclusive facts about The Goose Girl and The Artificial and other K.M. Robinson Series?

World Portals are now available on
www.kmrobinsonbooks.com

Learn behind the scenes facts, watch videos, play games, check out our book filters, find out where to get bonus scenes, view fan art, and get access to other secrets we've hidden away inside the World Portals on the website.

The World Portals are constantly changing and information is being taken away and added all the time, so check back frequently for new content!

ABOUT THE AUTHOR

K.M. Robinson is a storyteller who creates new worlds both in her writing and in her fine arts conceptual photography. She is a marketing, branding and social media strategy educator who is recognized at first sight by her very long hair. She is a creative who focuses on photography, videography, couture dress making, and writing to express the stories she needs to tell. She almost always has a camera within reach. Visit her at her website: www.kmrobinsonbooks.com

facebook.com/kmrobinsonbooks

instagram.com/kmrobinsonbooks

twitter.com/kmrobinsonbooks

Get free books and excerpts of other K.M. Robinson books at excerpt.kmrobinsonbooks.com

ALSO BY K.M. ROBINSON

The Jaded Duology

Book One: Jaded

Book Two: Risen

The Complete Series Boxset/Omnibus with exclusive epilogue

The Golden Trilogy

Book One: Golden

Forged: A Golden Novella

Book Two: Locked

Book Three: Edge

The Complete Series Boxset/Omnibus with exclusive bonus

novella, Tempered

The Siren Wars Saga

Book One: The Siren Wars

Book Two: Darker Depths

Book Three: Beyond The Shores

Book Four: Forbidden Waters (Coming in 2019)

Origins of the Siren Wars: Prequel Novella

The Legends Chronicles

Along Came A Spider: A Prequel Novelette

And They'll Come Home: A Prequel Novelette

The Archives of Jack Frost

The Revolution of Jack Frost

Virtually Sleeping Beauty: A Sleeping Beauty Novella Retelling

The Goose Girl and The Artificial: A Goose Girl Novella Retelling

The Sinking: A Little Mermaid Novella Retelling

Cindrill: A Cinderella Novella Retelling

Sugarcoated: A Hansel and Gretel's Witch Novella Retelling

JADED: BOOK ONE OF THE JADED DUOLOGY

Her father failed in his mission to take control from the Commander, a defeat that has cost Jade her life. She will die as punishment. Now she belongs to the Commander's son—as his wife. Knowing his intent is to quietly kill her in revenge, Jade's every move is calculated to survive—until she learns her death ensures the safety of her father and her entire town.

Roan doesn't want to kill Jade, but once his family isolates her from her father and community, his only choice is to go through with the plan. Jade doesn't make it easy as she tries to sway him into falling for her. Each misstep makes him question his cause. Each moment makes every decision harder, but the Commander won't allow him to fail.

One chooses life. One chooses death. In the midst of the chaos, only one will succeed.

Now available!
Learn more about The Jaded Duology at
jadedinfo.kmrobinsonbooks.com

GOLDEN: BOOK ONE OF THE GOLDEN TRILOGY

Goldilocks was never naive. She was sent on a mission and Dov Baer is her new target.

When the girl with the golden hair betrays everyone, not even she has hope of surviving.

The stories say that Goldilocks was a naïve girl who wandered into a house one day. Those stories were wrong. She was never naïve. It was all a perfectly executed plan to get her into the Baers' group to destroy them.

Trained by her cousin, Lowell, and handler, Shadoe, Auluria's mission is to destroy the Baers by getting close to the youngest brother, Dov, his brother and sister-in-law and the leaders of the Baers' group.

When she realizes Dov isn't as evil as her cousin led her to believe, she must figure out how to play both sides or her deception will cause everyone in her world to burn.

If her allegiances are discovered, either side could destroy her...if the Society doesn't get her first.

Available now!
Learn more about The Golden Trilogy at
goldeninfo.kmrobinsonbooks.com

**THE SIREN WARS: BOOK ONE OF THE
SIREN WARS SAGA**

War has hovered around the kingdom of Scylla for generations ever since the original sirens left the mer collection generations ago after nearly drowning the human prince. Over the years, select mermaids from the royal bloodline have been trained as spies to work for the reigning kings and queens, keeping the collection safe from sirens and humans.

Celena and her partner, Merrick, work covertly for the royals—not even her twin brother knows. When they discover the sirens have broken through the barriers the mer set up to keep the sirens out, Celena and her friends must race to the old kingdom of Metten to stop them from starting a war within their borders.

When she's dragged to the surface, Celena realizes that the war above the waters is as deadly as the one below the waves—and sacrificing herself may be the only way to protect her family.

The Siren Wars have only just begun.

Available now!
Learn more about The Siren Wars Saga at
sirenwarsinfo.kmrobinsonbooks.com

ALONG CAME A SPIDER: THE FIRST PREQUEL NOVELETTE TO THE LEGENDS CHRONICLES

Little Hacker Muffet
sat on her tuffet
destroying her cords and Way.
Along came a hacker named Spider,
who sat down beside her
and frightened his opponent away.

WHEN FET, ONE OF THE MOST SKILLED HACKERS IN THE Legends, discovers her best friend and leader of her group has been abducted and held for ransom, she must escape unnoticed and find Peep before it's too late.

When Spider, a new recruit training to join her hacker ring, slips out with her and claims to have a plan to save her friend, Fet is forced to bring him along. As she discovers he's not who he claims to be, she faces grave danger and learns just how deadly a spider bite can be.

Now available!
Learn more about The Legends Chronicles at
acasinfo.kmrobinsonbooks.com

VIRTUALLY SLEEPING BEAUTY

SHE MAY BE DOING BATTLE IN THE VIRTUAL WORLD, BUT IN the real world, they can't wake her up…

All Rora wants is to help people as class president, give her time to local charities, and quietly earn her way to the top level of the virtual reality system that the entire country uses without anyone noticing she's the second best player in the game.

All Royce wants to do is level up as a knight inside the gaming system, slay dragons, and eventually play his way to controlling the palace as he takes the crown away from the reigning queen.

When his Aunt Perry calls him, hysterically screaming that her goddaughter, Rora, has been inside for more than the four hours the game allows, Royce rushes over to help.

Entering the game, Royce soon discovers that Rora is trapped inside the system after an encounter with an evil magician who can change forms inside the game and control the virtual world. If he and his friend can't help her beat the game, she might not be able to wake up in the real world at all.

When virtual knights and princesses meet to slay dragons and defeat evil rulers, there's nothing stopping them from suffering real-world consequences too.

To wake her up, he must enter the game and help her beat it.

Now available!
Learn more about Virtually Sleeping Beauty at
vsbinfo.kmrobinsonbooks.com

THE REVOLUTION OF JACK FROST

No one inside the snow globe knows that Morozoko Industries is controlling their weather, testing them to form a stronger race that can survive the fall out from the bombs being dropped in the outside world—all they know is that they must survive the harsh Winter that lasts a month and use the few days of Spring, Summer, and Fall to gather enough supplies to survive.

When the seasons start shifting, Genesis and Jack know something is going on. As their team begins to find technology that they don't have access to inside their snow globe of a world, it begins to look more and more like one of their own is working against them.

. . .

Genesis soon discovers Morozoko Industries, but when a foreign enemy tries to destroy their weather program to make sure their destructive life-altering bombs succeed in destroying the outside world, only one person can shut down the machine that is spinning out of control and save the lives of everyone inside the bunker—Jack.

Now available!
Learn more about The Revolution of Jack Frost at
jackfrostinfo.kmrobinsonbooks.com

THE SINKING

The sea with wants to silence her, but not for the reason you think.

WHEN A QUIRKY OLDER WOMAN PAWNS A FANCY SEASHELL necklace at her mother's antique shop on the pier, Cara doesn't think much about the story the woman spins about the wearer turning into a mermaid.

On her way home, she accidentally drops the necklace into the ocean and is swept out to sea where she meets Quay--a merman who volunteers to take her to his mother, the sea queen, to help her get her legs back.

. . .

Cara soon learns that it's Quay's eighteen birthday--a day that has been a curse for his family--and is meant to be one for her too. Now she must fight to survive the sea with Quay at her side.

Fans of The Little Mermaid will love this twisted take on the beloved story.

Now available!
Learn more about The Sinking at
thesinkinginfo.kmrobinsonbooks.com

CINDRILL

It's hard to recognize a woman when she uses technology to change her appearance.

The nanobots Cindrill's master gave her allow her to slip around the kingdom and into the palace without being identified, but when she's injured by Prince Davian as she flees after an assassination attempt by her master, the prince realizes she's wearing the technology as a mask.

When Cindrill accidentally runs into the prince on his frantic search to find the would-be assassin woman, he doesn't recognize her without the nanobot mask on her face and insists she help in his search for the vile woman who tried to kill his father and nearly took away his fianceé.

Cindrill and Davian still have jobs to do while working together—*destroy each other*—and they have to play the game as long as they can until the other ruined, even as Cindrill's master takes matters into his own hands to finish the job they were hired to do.

Will her master and his betrothed get in the way of their survival?

Learn more about Cindrill at

cindrillinfo.kmrobinsonbooks.com

SUGARCOATED

Hansel and Gretel's witch was actually on their side…

Annika's job is to create a cake to match the candy-colored rooftops, nightly firework shows, and daily parades ending in unexpected executions for the mad king's ball, but her true mission is to sneak a thirteen-year-old assassin into the palace inside her cake using her gift of illusions.

Hansel's job is to protect his little sister, Gretel, once she assassinates King Levin and ends the destruction in Candestrachen, using his power over light to rescue the young girl from the chaos her influence over life and death will create.

. . .

When the entire forest reconstructs itself under Gretel's command while trying to save herself from a king's guard, Hansel and Annika must put their feelings aside and ensure their plan holds true—even if it means one of them has to sacrifice themselves to protect the mission.

Her illusions were meant to save her....but not everyone will survive the assassination attempt.

Learn more about Sugarcoated at
sugarcoatedinfo.kmrobinsonbooks.com

www.ingramcontent.com/pod-product-compliance
Lightning Source LLC
Chambersburg PA
CBHW032043180726
48284CB00008B/2725